Published by Modern Publishing
A Division of Unisystems, Inc.

Printed in Italy.

WINSTON'S
RED BOOTS

Written and Illustrated by Frank and Carol Hill

MODERN PUBLISHING
A Division of Unisystems, Inc.
New York, New York 10022

Winston Walrus was up in his attic looking for his tennis racquet when he stumbled upon his Uncle Bluewhiskers' old red pirate boots.

When Winston tried them on, one of the toes popped open and out fell a treasure map! "This way to the gold," Winston read aloud.

Winston ran downstairs and phoned his friend Saul.
"Forget tennis," he said, "I've got something that's much
more fun to do. It's treasure hunting. Meet me at the wharf
in ten minutes."

The directions from the wharf were easy — paddle due north for five minutes as fast as you can. "This must be the buried treasure my Uncle Bluewhiskers is always talking about. He lost the map years ago," explained Winston.

When they reached the place where "X" marked the spot on the map, they could see an old shipwreck way down below.

With a big splash, Winston and Saul jumped into the
water and swam toward the ship.

There sitting right in the middle of the ship was the ancient pirate chest. They eagerly yanked it open . . .

. . . and found the most shiny, brilliant goldfish, which Winston immediately recognized as his Uncle Bluewhiskers' favorite pet!

"So that's what Uncle Bluewhiskers meant," laughed Winston, "when he said he'd misplaced his Bullion. That's the name of his pet goldfish."

Saul and Winston returned to their boat with Bullion and paddled back to the wharf. "Gee, won't Uncle Bluewhiskers be glad to see you," said Winston.

As they walked down the path leading home, they heard a
friendly voice calling from the woods.

It was Uncle Bluewhiskers. He thanked Winston and Saul for finding Bullion and gave each of them a big gold coin.

"Wow! Treasure after all!" exclaimed Winston as he and Saul ran off to treat themselves to their favorite ice cream cones as a reward for their hard day of treasure hunting.